Dec 25 1999

Happy Birthday to Our Christmas Angel

Love

Pop + Me ()

Angel Food

Written by Starr Hall
Illustrated by Mari M. Robeson

Simply Angels™
P.O. Box 644
Cambria, CA 93428
(800) 914-7577

Simply Angels™
P.O. Box 644
Cambria, CA 93428
(800) 914-7577
e-mail simply.angels@thegrid.net

Text © 1996 by Starr Hall Atiyeh.
Illustrations © by Mari M. Robeson.

Library of Congress Catalog Card Number 96-092690

Book and cover design by Mari M. Robeson

Edited by Grady Hall
Book layout by Woody Hall
Printed in the USA
Printed by Print & Bindery
A Division of Artis, Inc. Buellton, CA

ISBN 0-9651678-2-8
$15.95

Other books in print by Simply Angels™
"Where Do Angels By Their Clothes?

I would like to dedicate this book to the two most wonderful imaginative Angels, my children, Austin, and Savannah. They constantly remind me to Wake Up and Smell the Fun! With a loving thanks to my mother Heidi, and also to an angel that has recently re-entered my life. Thank you for your love and support. I love you all!

"Angel Food" would not have been possible without the editing and brainstorming help by my brother, Grady Hall, a gifted writer himself. The story was brought to life visually by Mari M. Robeson with her wonderful imaginative Illustrations. I would also like to thank my brother, Woody Hall for giving up his weekends to help layout this book. I send my deepest thanks to Grady, Mari, and Woody for putting their love and time into "Angel Food", and to everyone else who has helped me along the way in bringing "Angel Food" into this world.

With Love To You,

Starr Hall

It's impossible for me to dedicate this book to one person, because during the days it took to complete these illustrations, three people put their lives on hold. Their constant support, love and care of my little girl, Serena, allowed me the time to create. With love and gratitude to my husband, Bill Robeson, and parents, Frank and Ethel Monforte.

Mari M. Robeson

1

It was an ordinary night
when I sat down to eat.
As mommy lowered my plate,
I settled in my seat.

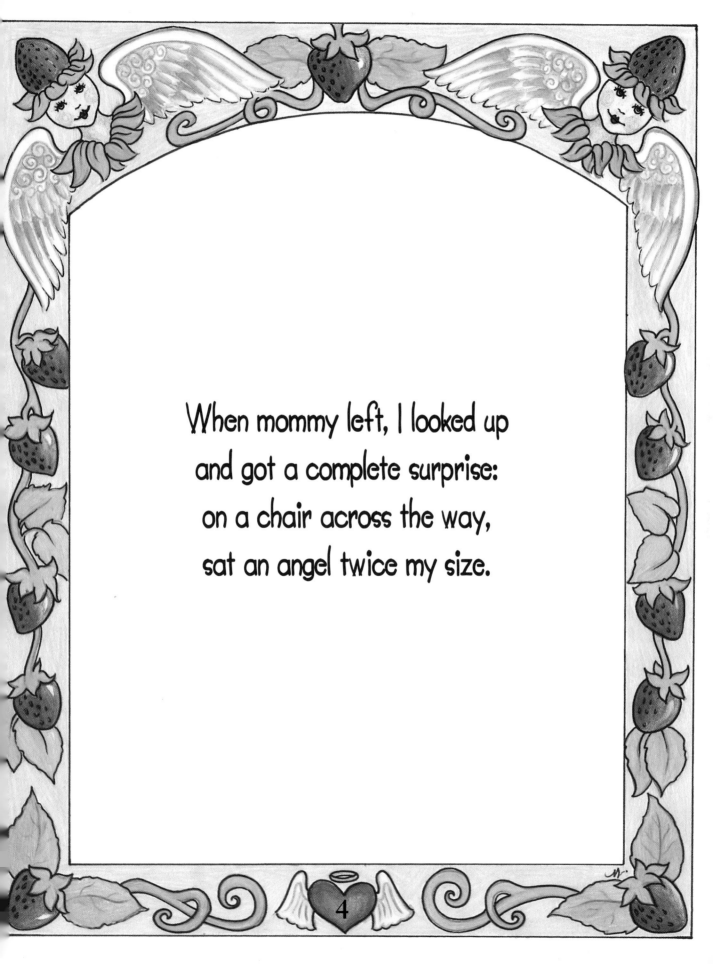

When mommy left, I looked up
and got a complete surprise:
on a chair across the way,
sat an angel twice my size.

4

5

"Hello, I'm Marissa," she said,
as she plopped down with a sigh.
"I'm so hungry I could eat a horse,
but I'll settle for apple pie."

Mom didn't spot the angel,
because she had to answer the phone.
So I turned to talk with Marissa,
as we were all alone.

Marissa picked up a napkin
and looked over all our food.
"Angels don't get hungry," I giggled,
trying not to be rude.
"Of course we get hungry, silly.
Food helps our halos shine bright.
A glowing halo and happy wings,
are just what we need for flight."

"But all we have here is grown-up food,
like broccoli and squishy tomatoes.
Why, we can't even have the fruit salad,
until we eat our mashed potatoes.
This food doesn't always taste good,
though mom says it's nutritious.
But I like sweet candies best,
because they're quite delicious."

13

"Our halos won't light without
grown-up food,
but it takes more than that to fly.
If we want to use our wings,
then it's Angel Food we try."

15

"Angel Food?" I asked, confused,
"Is that something that you can bake?
Like sugar cookies and pies,
or a chocolate pudding cake?"

"Do you get it from a restaurant,
or can you buy it at the store?
Can you grow it in the garden
if you need to get some more?"

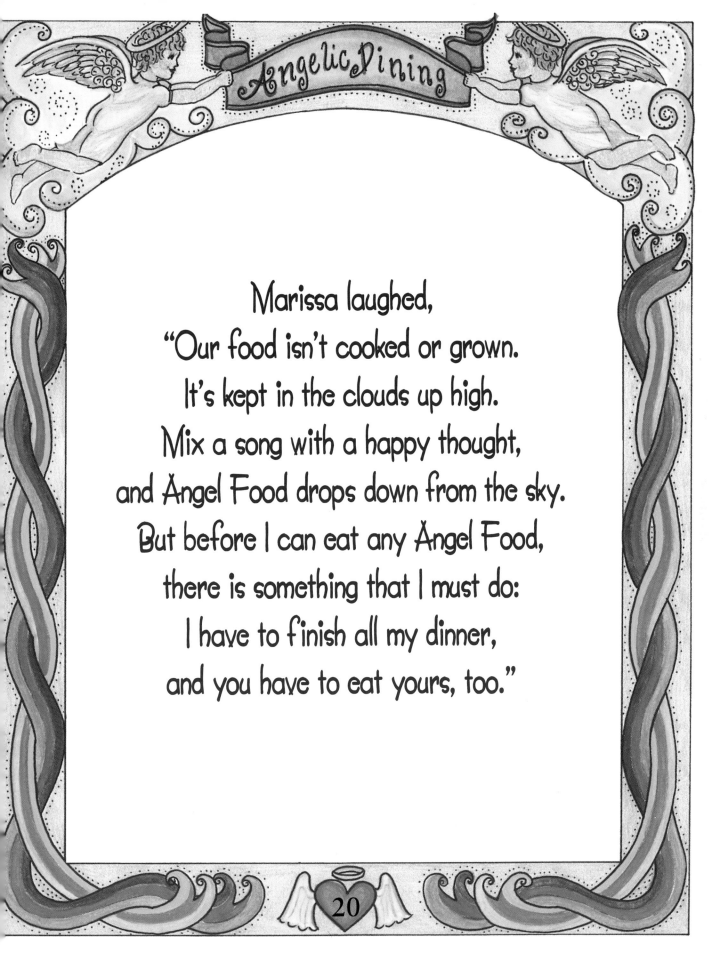

Marissa laughed,
"Our food isn't cooked or grown.
It's kept in the clouds up high.
Mix a song with a happy thought,
and Angel Food drops down from the sky.
But before I can eat any Angel Food,
there is something that I must do:
I have to finish all my dinner,
and you have to eat yours, too."

21

Marissa ate her food so quickly,
that I could barely finish mine.
And when I looked over, I noticed
her halo had a brighter shine.

23

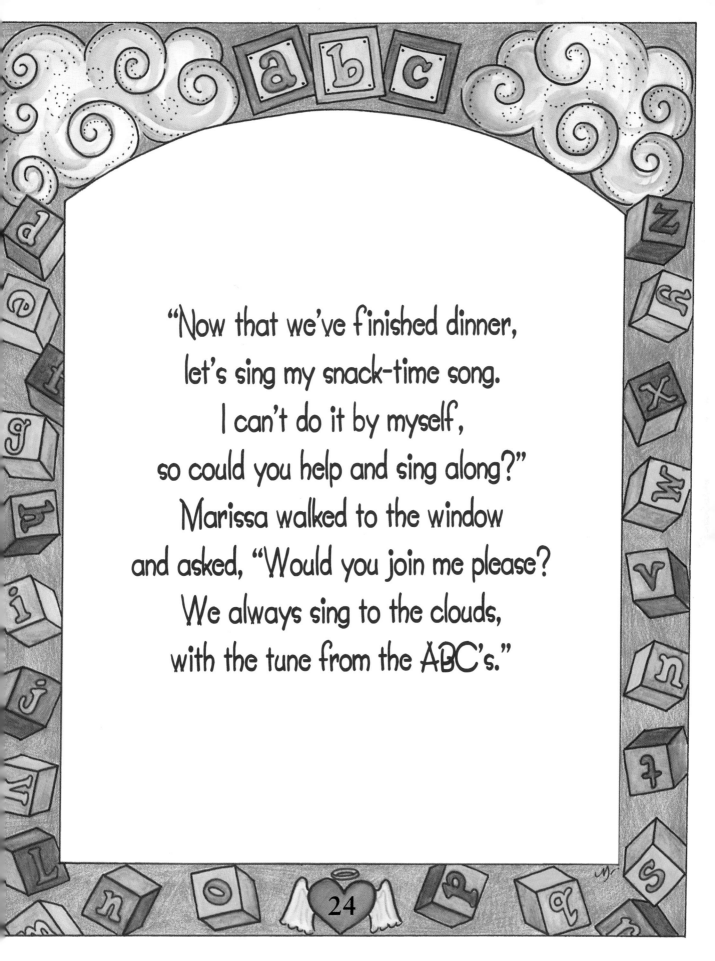

"Now that we've finished dinner,
let's sing my snack-time song.
I can't do it by myself,
so could you help and sing along?"
Marissa walked to the window
and asked, "Would you join me please?
We always sing to the clouds,
with the tune from the ABC's."

"You can't sing at dinner," I said,
to Marissa across the way.
"Dinner is the time to eat,
and we only sing at play."
"It's always time to play," she said,
"but we don't need to shout or yell.
We'll just sing the song softly,
and no one could ever tell."

26

27

With that, Marissa whispered
the words into my ear.
"Now let's sing it quietly,
so your mom doesn't hear":
CLOUD CONES, CLOUD CONES,
SUNBERRY PIE.
RAINBOW RINGS AND STARS UP HIGH.
MOON COOKIES AND
BRIGHT-CRACKER STARS.
THUNDER PUFFS AND
LIGHTNING-BOLT BARS.
WON'T YOU SEND ME SNACKS TO EAT?
IT WOULD BE A DELIGHTFUL TREAT!

29

As the food drifted in the window,
after it came down from the sky,
I watched Marissa stuff her face,
with cloud cones and sunberry pie.

31

The Angel Food disappeared
when it began to hit the floor.
I'm glad that it stopped there,
because we couldn't eat anymore.

33

"It's time for me to go now,"
Marissa stood up to say.
She tipped her halo, fluffed her wings,
then turned and flew away.

I watched her fly out the window
and then I walked down the hall.
I stopped to look in the mirror,
we had hanging on the wall.

There I saw a halo,
shining bright above my head!
Is this what happens
when you don't eat sweets,
and eat grown-up food instead?

Starr Hall

Starr Hall has been rhyming her thoughts and creative stories since she was 9 years old. With the love and support of her family and friends in 1995, she finally decided to bring her stories to life and help children in using their imagination. Starr has a lifetime of stories to write (and rhyme!) and can be found working on them in beautiful seaside Cambria, California where she lives with her two children.

Mari M. Robeson

Mari Robeson has always had a passion for the arts. In 1986 she graduated with her Bachelor of Science degree in Art and Design from Cal Poly State University, San Luis Obispo, CA. Soon after, she went to work for a large corporation, where she handled Advertising and Visual Designs for several years. But after the birth of her daughter, Serena, in 1995, she shifted focus onto pursuing a career that would allow her more time with her family as well as follow her true love for illustrating. It was then that she opened Le Sol Design Studio in beautiful San Luis Obispo, CA.

Much of Mari Robeson's success is based on hard work and all the wonderful support she receives from her family and friends. She would like to thank Starr Hall and Heidi Borchers for this wonderful, creative opportunity. She would also like to thank her two models, Jesikah Stolaroff (little girl) and Kamron Lorencz (Angel) who are both real life Angels.

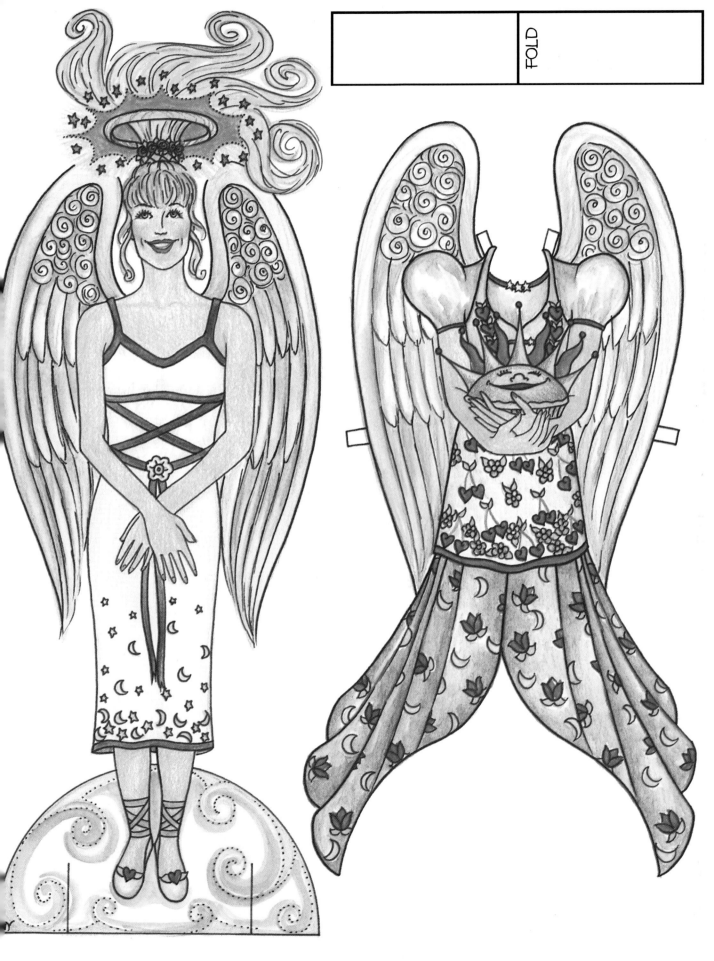

FOLD

FOLD